It's a Perfect Night

It's a Perfect Night

Abigail Pizer

MACMILLAN CHILDREN'S BOOKS

First published 1994 by
Macmillan Children's Books
an imprint of Macmillan Publishers Limited
a division of Macmillan Limited
Cavaye Place London SW10 9PG
and Basingstoke
Associated companies worldwide

This edition first published 1995

ISBN 0 333 63755 0

9 8 7 6 5 4 3 2 1

A CIP catalogue record for this book is available
from the British Library.

Printed in Hong Kong

As the sun sets behind the woods . . .

the night animals begin to stir.

It's the perfect night to call his friends,
thought the frog.

Croak, croak!

The  says Croak, croak!

What a perfect night!

It's the perfect night to catch insects,
thought the bat.

Squeak, squeak!

The says Croak, croak!

The says Squeak, squeak!

What a perfect night!

It’s the perfect night to look for slugs,
thought the hedgehog.

Snuffle, snuffle!

The says Croak, croak!

The says Squeak, squeak!

The says Snuffle, snuffle!

What a perfect night!

It's the perfect night to sing her song,
thought the nightjar.

Churr, churr!

The  says Croak, croak!

The says Squeak, squeak!

The says Snuffle, snuffle!

The says Churr, churr!

What a perfect night!

It's the perfect night for a swim in a stream,
thought the mink.

Hiss, hiss!

The says Croak, croak!

The says Squeak, squeak!

The says Snuffle, snuffle!

The says Churr, churr!

The says Hiss, hiss!

What a perfect night!

It's the perfect night to hunt for mice,
thought the cat.

Meow, meow!

The [frog] says Croak, croak!

The [bat] says Squeak, squeak!

The [hedgehog] says Snuffle, snuffle!

The [bird] says Churr, churr!

The [animal] says Hiss, hiss!

The [cat] says Meow, meow!

What a perfect night!

It's the perfect night to visit the graveyard,
thought the owl.

Hoot, hoot!

The  says Croak, croak!

The says Squeak, squeak!

The says Snuffle, snuffle!

The says Churr, churr!

The says Hiss, hiss!

The says Meow, meow!

The says Hoot, hoot!

What a perfect night!

It's the perfect night to look for leftovers,
thought the fox.

Bark, bark!

The says Croak, croak!

The says Squeak, squeak!

The says Snuffle, snuffle!

The says Churr, churr!

The says Hiss, hiss!

The says Meow, meow!

The says Hoot, hoot!

The says Bark, bark!

What a perfect night!

It's the perfect night to take her young for a walk, thought the shrew.

Eek, eek!

The says Croak, croak!

The says Squeak, squeak!

The says Snuffle, snuffle!

The says Churr, churr!

The says Hiss, hiss!

The says Meow, meow!

The says Hoot, hoot!

The says Bark, bark!

The says Eek, eek!

What a perfect night!

It's the perfect night to chew some grass,
thought the rabbit.

Munch, munch!

That was a perfect night!

Also by Abigail Pizer

IT'S A PERFECT DAY
LOPPYLUGS
NOSEY GILBERT
HENRIETTA GOOSE
WHAT HAPPENED TO WILFRED BEAR
TIPPU

Other Macmillan books you will enjoy

SWEETIE Jonathan Allen
KING OF THE WOODS Ken Brown and David Day
FRUIT BAT Mark Foreman
ME FIRST Helen Lester and Lynn Munsinger
THE FOXBURY FORCE Graham Oakley
I WISH I WERE BIG Gerald Rose
ELIZABETH, LARRY AND ED Marilyn Sadler and Roger Bollen
BUT WHAT DOES THE HIPPOPOTAMUS SAY? Francesca Simon and Helen Floate
THE WITNESS Robert Westall and Sophy Williams

For a complete list of Macmillan children's books write to

Macmillan Children's Books
18–21 Cavaye Place
London SW10 9PG